March 3, 1993

Tawny
Scrawny Lion
Saves the Day

By Michael Teitelba[...]
Illustrated by Art and K[...]

D0605115

A GOLDEN BOOK • NEW YORK
Western Publishing Company, Inc., Racine, Wisconsin 53404

There is a magical place called Little Golden Book Land, filled with wonderful things to see and do. Every day is a special day, just waiting to be discovered.

One afternoon in Little Golden Book Land
Tawny Scrawny Lion was visiting some of his
rabbit friends.

"I'm hungry," roared Tawny Scrawny Lion.
"Let's make a big hot potful of carrot stew."

The rabbits agreed. "We'll go collect the
berries and vegetables we need to make the
stew," one fat little rabbit said. "Tawny, you can
stay here and set the table. We'll be back in no
time at all."

The rabbits wandered through the woods, collecting berries and vegetables. "I found a beautiful bunch of carrots," said the fat little rabbit.

Soon they came to a powerful rushing river. At the end of a fallen tree that stuck out into the river was a bunch of stew berries—the very best kind of berries for making carrot stew.

"Oh, we must get those stew berries!" exclaimed the biggest rabbit. "They are so hard to find." With that, the rabbits walked out to the end of the fallen tree.

Then, just as the last of the rabbits reached the berries, they heard a terrible cracking sound. The tree broke loose from the shore and was swept off by the rushing river, carrying the rabbits with it.

"Help!" they cried, but there was no one to hear their shouts.

Meanwhile, back at the rabbits' house, Tawny Scrawny Lion was getting very worried. The rabbits had been gone for a very long time. "I hope nothing has happened," he thought. "I'd better go and find them!"

He called on his friend Poky Little Puppy to
help him track the rabbits through the woods.
Poky Little Puppy had a great sense of smell, and
they were soon following the path the rabbits
had taken.

"Look! There they are!" shouted Tawny Scrawny Lion as he spotted the rabbits.

"They're stuck on that tree in the middle of the river!" cried Poky Little Puppy. "And the tree is stuck on some rocks!"

"Help! Help!" shouted the frightened rabbits.

"Tawny, will you be able to swim out there to rescue them?" asked Poky Little Puppy.

"No," he replied. "The current here is much too strong even for me."

Tawny Scrawny Lion was very upset. Suddenly
he had an idea. "You wait here," he said to
Poky Little Puppy. "I'm going to get help."

Tawny Scrawny Lion raced through the Jolly
Jungle until he found his friend Saggy Baggy
Elephant. He explained what had happened and
his plan for rescuing the rabbits.

When they returned to the river, Saggy Baggy
Elephant sprang into action. "This is the biggest
tree I could find," he said as he lifted it with his
trunk. "I only hope it's long enough to reach the
rabbits. They could climb over it to shore."

Saggy Baggy Elephant carried the tree to the shore and placed it in the river. Although it was the longest tree around, it was still too short to reach the rabbits.

"Oh, no!" cried Tawny Scrawny Lion. "I was sure that would work. Now what are we going to do?"

Just then Baby Brown Bear showed up. He had heard shouting, and he came to see what it was all about. "I'm a pretty good climber," he said. "Maybe I can climb out to the end of the tree and try to reach the rabbits."

Baby Brown Bear climbed out to the end of the tree. He moved very carefully, because he did not want to fall into the river himself. When he got to the end, he reached out his paw, stretching his arm as far as he could. But his arm was just not long enough. "It's no use," he said. "They're too far away."

Tawny Scrawny Lion's face grew serious. "You're going to be all right!" he called to the rabbits. "I have another plan. Just stay calm. I'll be back as soon as I can." Then he turned and raced off at top speed.

Tawny Scrawny Lion ran to the nearest train station. He looked down the track and spotted Tootle and Katy Caboose, chugging along. "Tootle," he shouted. "I need your help! Stop! Please, stop!"

Tootle slammed on his brakes and came to a screeching halt. He was always glad to help his friend Tawny Scrawny Lion.

After Tawny Scrawny Lion explained the situation, Tootle said, "What are we waiting for? Hop on." The powerful engine was soon speeding along the tracks as fast as he could. He flew all the way into town and headed straight for the harbor.

There, Tawny Scrawny Lion found Scuffy the
tugboat. "I need your help," he said as he
brought an extra cargo car to the water and
began to fill it. "I'll explain on the way."

He pulled Scuffy into the cargo car and they
were off, racing back to the Jolly Jungle.

Back at the river, things had gone from bad to worse. The rabbits were now soaked to the bone, and a strong wind was blowing. They were hanging on to the tree for their lives.

"Do you think you can do it?" Tawny Scrawny
Lion asked Scuffy as he placed him in the water.
"I think so," replied Scuffy.
Using all of his power, Scuffy fought the
current and made his way to the rabbits.

Then, one at a time, they climbed aboard Scuffy. Battling the current again, he brought each rabbit safely to shore.

"Hurray!" all the friends cheered when the last rabbit was back on land.

"I don't know what we would have done if you hadn't come looking for us, Tawny," said the fat little rabbit. "You really saved the day."

"Everybody helped," said Tawny Scrawny Lion
modestly. "And the important thing is that my
rabbit friends are safe."

"Look," said the biggest rabbit. "I got the stew
berries."

Everyone smiled. Then Tootle took them all
back home to the rabbits' house for a warm
dinner of carrot stew.